TO OUR beloved
LUCY

You are the
sparkle of our
home xoxo

In a tiny house in a town nestled in the countryside, there lived four happy and cheerful dogs having the best time of their lives. Among them was Lucy, the most mischievous and lively of them all.

So, on a rainy day, when Mom and Dad weren't so keen on walking the four dogs in the mud and rain, Lucy sat by the window and looked at the trees marking the edge of the forest. Lucy looked sad, so her siblings came and tried to cheer her up one by one.

First came Bailey with Lucy's tennis ball. It's her favorite toy and if left alone with it, she can play with it for days. So, Bailey found it very strange when Lucy dismissed the ball without even giving it a good thump and a chase.

Next came Bobby, who with his high energy can encourage anyone to join in with him on some high-speed fun. But not Lucy, not today.

And lastly, came Dilly who thought it best to sit down and instead have a chat. She laid down next to her sister and asked, "What's wrong, Lucy? You don't want to come and play with us?"

Lucy felt gloomy, but just when Dilly left, the rain stopped and the curious beagle saw something that caught her interest. Dad had just gone to take some trash outside, but as he left, he slipped on a bit of wet grass and forgot to shut the door.

Lucy wouldn't normally pay attention to this, but today it was exactly what she needed for one of her master escape plans. So, she got up and slowly moved to greet Dad as he came back in.

Staying hidden just near the door, Lucy grabbed a shoe in her mouth and waited for the perfect moment. As Dad came back in Lucy, placed the shoe in the door to stop it from closing.

"Lets go!" Lucy made a run for the forest and quickly disappeared among the trees.

"Lucy, wait, where are you going? Lucy come back!!!" Bailey, Dilly and Bobby called out, but the adventurous beagle was at the start of the adventure of a lifetime. She had no intention of turning back, so they decided to follow her.

In the forest, there were so many things to see and smell, that the dogs forgot about all their worries and enjoyed the moment. After a while, Lucy heard a loud burble in the distance and called her siblings to follow her.

As they got closer to the sound, the dogs discovered a shallow river with perfectly clear water. So, they quickly jumped in and started to splash around. Lucy, Bobby, Dilly and Bailey never had so much fun!

After playing in the water, the dogs were exhausted. So, they got out and had a good shake-off. The water must have cooled their heads because the first thing Dilly said was that they should go back home.

But the paths of the forest all looked the same, they were lost and didn't know the right way. The sun was starting to set behind them, and the forest was getting darker by the second. Now their laughter and happy barks turned into whimpers and rumbling tummies.

"We'll never find our way home!" they all said
Lucy started to cry.

"I'm so sorry, guys," Lucy said with tears in her eyes. "It's all my fault. I thought all I wanted was an adventure, but it wasn't the same without Mom and Dad around. They are probably annoyed and so scared right now. It was a silly idea to run away."

The four dogs did just that and they quickly found the trail. They didn't see their house anywhere, but they knew they were close.

Suddenly, Lucy heard some familiar voices.
"Lucy! Bailey! Dilly! Bobby!"

Mom and Dad were on the trail!

Back home Mom and Dad gave the four escape artists a bath, some food, and a lot of cuddles. Lucy was happy she went on a great adventure, but she won't be so quick to run away again.

Printed in Great Britain
by Amazon